ZEBRA
MILKSHAKES
+
GIANT CARROTS

THE ADVENTURES OF

DEVIL-CAT

VOLUME 3

MAIN CHARACTERS

DEVIL-CAT

Pizza-lover
Chaos-causer
Master-burglar

General,
all-round villain

The **GREATEST** criminal
ever!

Dear reader-person,

Welcome to the **third volume** of my *brilliant* and *exciting* stories.

Did you know that am I *The World's Greatest Criminal*?

Yes, of course you knew that.

Everyone knows that.

This book has two stories in it, each as *unbelievable* as the other. The first is about a milkshake factory, the second is about vegetables.

Happy reading!

- Devil Cat
  (Master Criminal)

www.**itsdevilcat**.com

BORING STUFF

SERIOUSLY DULL!

Age: Unknown

Height: 5 ft (incl. ears)
Weight: 122 lbs (55 kgs)
Number of tails: 2

Favourite food: Pizza, carrots, sardine-flavoured ice-cream

Favourite drinks: Smiley-cola, Shakey Mc-Shake Shakes, carrot juice

Terrified of: Watermelons
Main hobby: Sleeping
Hours of sleep per day: 16

BUNNY-FACE

Devil-Cat's *arch-enemy*
CRAFTY, *Patient*

Age: Unknown
Height: 4ft (including ears)
Weight: 110 lbs (49 kgs)
Number of tails: 1

Favourite food: *Everything*
Favourite drink: Smiley-cola

Terrified of: Falling cakes
Main hobby: Watching TV
Hours of sleep per day: 12

THE BALD BOG-SLOTNIGG BROTHERS

* Friends of Bunny-Face
* Twins
* **Not** *super-smart*

Age: Unknown
Height: 5ft
Weight: Bruno 165 lbs (75 kgs)
Boris 174 lbs (79 kgs)

Number of tails: We haven't checked but *zero* we imagine!

Favourite food: Maggot pie
Favourite drink: Smiley-cola

Terrified of: Cockroaches
Main hobby: Art
Hours of sleep per day: Unknown

Story 1

Zebra Milkshakes

This is the local
milkshake factory.

Makers of the much-loved
Shakey-McShake-Shakes.

This is Mr. McVash, the much-loved owner of the factory.

It was he who invented the Shakey-McShake-Shake recipe (which is why he is much-loved).

Shakey-McShake-Shakes are TOTALLY delicious.

Everyone agrees, including: The President,

Mrs. Clamfinch,*

Owner of the Smiley-Cola factory (Vol 2, p12)

The Bog-Slotnigg Brothers,

Bunny-Face,

And, of course, Devil-Cat himself!

Devil-Cat went online to find the recipe.

The Shakey-McShake -Shake recipe is TOP secret.

Devil-Cat grabbed his telescope and faced it towards the factory.

Luck was on Devil-Cat's side. He spotted the safe-room!

Think Devil-Cat, think!

So Devil-Cat went out and bought a Shakey-McShake -Shake.

So Devil-Cat went online to buy a cow.

So Devil-Cat sat down at his desk again.

② BorroW A HorSe FroM THe H.L.S. (HorSe LeNDiNG SOCieTy)

③ THeN juST RiDE TO a NEARBy FaRM...

Pimple
(with dimple)

So Devil-Cat did exactly that: He dressed up as a cowboy...

...got a horse and rode to a nearby farm.

But when the cows saw him...

But it was no good. He couldn't get anywhere near the cows.

Then the farmer arrived.

43

Devil-Cat rode home
dejected and empty-handed.

Turned out not to be so
simple as a pimple with a
dimple after all,
did it Devil-Cat?

Devil-Cat got back to work.

① DRESS UP AS AN ACTUAL COW.

② GO TO A NEARBY FARM

NEARBY FARM

So Devil-Cat did just that. He dressed up as a cow.

And then headed over to another nearby farm.

Devil-Cat headed home dejected.

STEAL ONE USING A CGD (COW-GRABBING DRONE)

As straightforward a plan as a man with a tan called Stan, in a van (with a fan) and a wife called Anne.

STAN'S VACUUM CLEANERS AND DENTAL SUPPLIES

Or was it Suzanne?
Or Dianne?

Or Joanne?

Anyway...

Devil-Cat went to the drone shop and left with a Cow-Grabbing Drone.

He then sent the drone over to a nearby farm.

And grabbed a cow!

But she was too heavy.

...onto a tree!

The cow was totally confused.

65

He called the
fire-department.

Who came...

...and rescued the cow.

WE'RE USED TO GETTING CATS OUT OF TREES, BUT NEVER A COW!

This really was NOT as straightforward a plan as a man with a tan called Stan, in a van (with a fan) and a wife named Anne. Or Suzanne or Dianne or even Joanne.

Devil-Cat was REALLY dejected, and about to give up.

But he then thought of the milkshakes, *and cheered up.*

Now he was determined.

Think Devil-Cat, think.

And with those thoughts still swishing around in his head, more determined than ever, Devil-Cat sat down to write again.

In case you didn't know it, Zebra-Paint is an extraordinary paint that comes out in black and white stripes.

② SNeAk iNTO A NEARBy FaRM At NiGHT.

③ PAiNt a SLeePiNG cow TO LOOk LiKE A ZeBRA.

④ THEN rIDE OUT ON iT.

⑤ ANyONE WHO SeeS A caT RidING A ZEbRA WiLL JuSt THiNK tHEy ArE IMaGINING It And Go HoMe to BEd!!

So Devil-Cat did exactly that. He went and bought some paint.

74

Then he went to yet another nearby farm.

He found a cow that was fast asleep.

He painted it to look like a zebra.

Once he was done, he tried to wake it up, but couldn't.

He climbed on top of it
and started whispering.

The cow opened an eye.

Then looked down at itself and thought: "I'm a zebra, and someone is whispering to me! He's telling me it's time for a walk."

And out rode Devil-Cat.

All the way back to his house.

Once inside though, the cow suddenly realised it was not a dream.

And that's how Devil-Cat got the cow to stay.

BUT, later, when Devil-Cat
tried to remove the paint,
it wouldn't come off.

And then Devil-cat got to work. He milked the cow.

And started experimenting with milkshakes.

Soon he was making good progress.

Better and better every day!

The cow was very happy.

Eventually Devil-Cat tested one of his shakes on the Bog-Slotnigg brothers.

And so he started selling them.

People liked them.

A lot!

Meanwhile the angry farmer was searching everywhere for his missing cow.

The farmer went walking off, looking for his cow.

Meanwhile, Devil-Cat had a *GENIUS* idea.

He re-painted his house and put up a sign!

People LOVED it.

ZEBRA SHAKES!!

ME WANT!!

Business was
BOOMING!

Bunny-Face came by to see what the fuss was all about.

But when he saw his arch-enemy Devil-Cat doing so well, he got rather jealous.

GRRRR

I'M GOING TO MAKE MY OWN ZEBRA-SHAKES, AND DRIVE DEVIL-CAT OUT OF BUSINESS.

Ooooo

So Bunny-Face got to work.

ALLIGATORS!

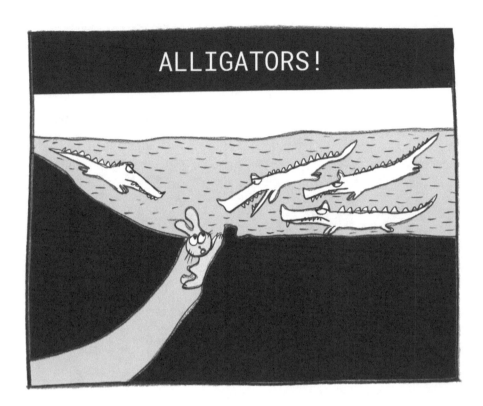

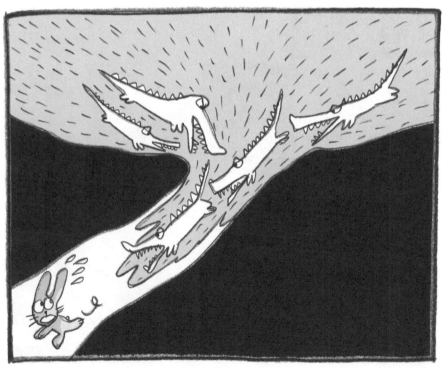

Bunny-Face *just* managed to escape.

① GEt A Huge Hot aIR BALLOOn.

② FLy OVeR tHE ZOO WaLL.

112

Up and away!

Homeward bound!

But no, the zebras were TOO HEAVY! They suddenly started losing height!

The Zoo Director had absolutely NO IDEA what was going on.

And that's when he had a
MOST BRILLIANT idea!

He rushed home and
quickly wrote it down.

② go to the zoo Director's House

③ And offer to get the zebras down from the roof.

④ THEN INSTEAD of TAKING THEM BACK to THE ZOO, SECRETLY BRING THEM to MY House!

So he put on his Z.R.S. outfit.

And went over to the Zoo Director's house.

Of course she immediately said YES to his offer of help.

Bunny-Face started building a slide from the roof.

But instead of it going back into the zoo, he *sneakily* *redirected* the slide over the zoo fence, towards his house!

Down went all the zebras!

Success **at last!**

The Zoo Director was now *REALLY* furious.

Back at home, Bunny-Face found the zebras **impossible** to milk.

And they were making a
mess of his house.

Bunny-Face was NOT happy.

But then Bunny-Face had his penny-drop moment. Maybe HIS zebras were not milkable but he knew ONE that DEFINITELY was. And that was DEVIL-CAT'S!

I NEED TO STEAL IT!

① TO STEAL DEViL-CAt's ActUAL ZEBRA...

② I GET some PAiNt...

③ ... tHEN go over to DEVil-CaT's PLACE.

④ THeN SNeaK iN and PAiNt THE ZEBrA to LooK LiKe a COW!

A few hours later, over at Devil-Cat's place, there was **A LOT** of snoring going on.

He was SO exhausted from running his **thriving** business that he didn't notice Bunny-Face sneaking in.

Luckily, the "zebra" was also exhausted.

Bunny-Face stood back and admired his paint-work.

Devil-Cat was still fast asleep and so didn't notice anything.

But the farmer DID!

He called the police.

Bunny-Face was arrested.

The farmer and the cow were reunited!

I MISSED YOU !!

The next morning Devil-Cat saw news of the reunion on TV.

He was actually relieved as he was getting bored (and tired) of making milkshakes.

He was so happy that he decided to go for a little stroll.

It was then that he heard the bleating.

He followed it.

All the way to Bunny-Face's house.

He saw the zebras trapped inside.

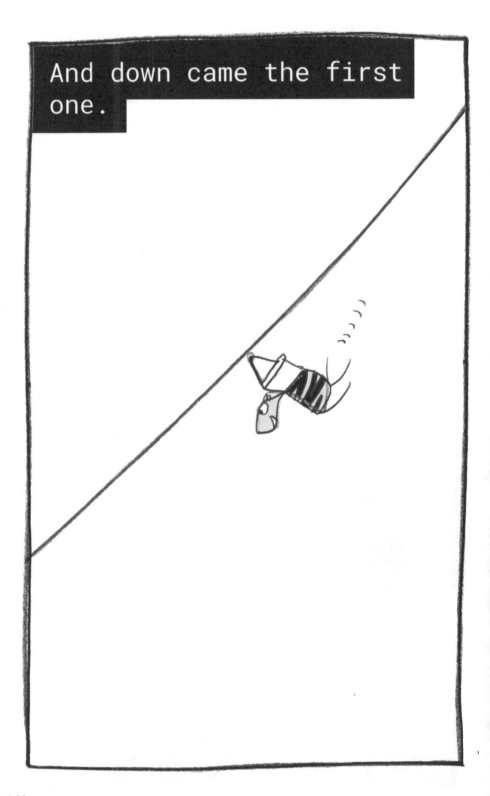

And down came the first one.

People came running.

Soon there was a crowd.

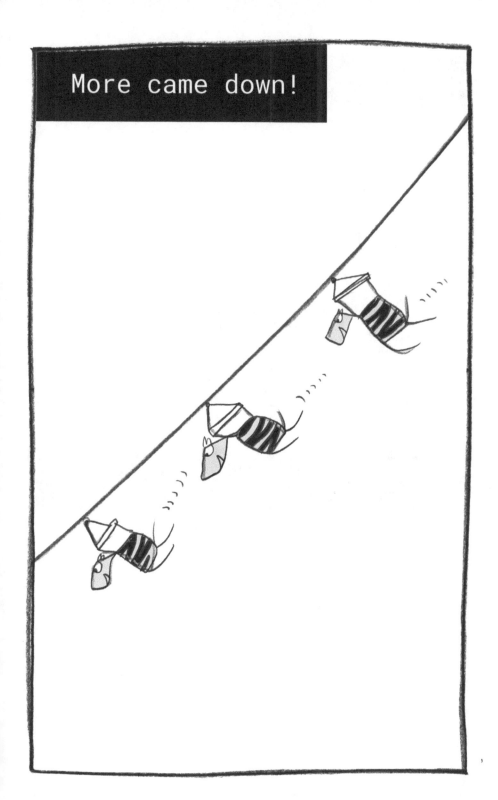

The crowd went CRAZY!

The Zoo Director arrived.

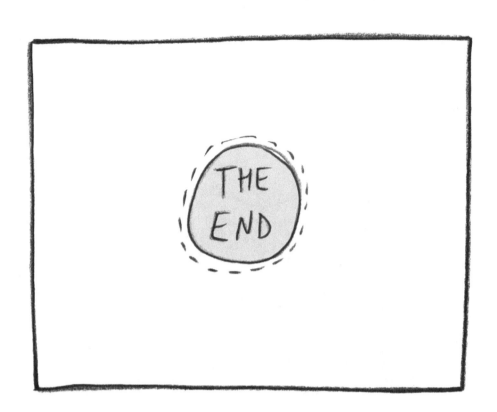

Story 2

The Battle of the CARROTS

LOTS OF EXCITEMENT IN TOWN TODAY BECAUSE...

IT'S THAT TIME OF YEAR FOR THE WORLD CARROT-GROWING CHAMPIONSHIPS.

WCGC

YOU'VE OBVIOUSLY HEARD ABOUT THIS EVENT.
BUT JUST TO REFRESH YOUR MEMORY, HERE ARE SOME DETAILS:

EACH ENTRANT IS GIVEN A PLOT OF LAND.

THEY THEN HAVE EXACTLY A MONTH TO GROW THEIR CARROT.

PLOT #144

ON THE FINAL DAY THEY PICK THEM...

PLOT #144

... AND PRESENTS A BUNCH OF PRIZES.

FOR THE WEIRDEST CARROT.

165

THE ONE THAT EVERYONE WAITS FOR.

THE CAMERAS ARE READY.

THE PRIZE FOR THE LARGEST CARROT!

AND IT'S NOT JUST A TROPHY, IT'S ALSO A FREE LIFETIME SUPPLY OF CARROT SANDWICHES.

AS YOU CAN IMAGINE, IT'S A BIG DEAL.

CARROT SANDWICHES, IN CASE YOU'VE FORGOTTEN, ARE MADE UP OF A CARROT BETWEEN TWO OTHER CARROTS.

THEY'RE DELICIOUS.

AND OBVIOUSLY HE WANTS TO WIN THE GRAND- PRIZE !!

LAST YEAR HE DIDN'T DO VERY WELL. IN FACT HE DIDN'T EVEN COME IN THE TOP TEN!

MEANWHILE, BUNNY-FACE, <u>BEING</u> A <u>BUNNY</u>, ALSO <u>LOVES</u> CARROTS.

SO ALSO ENTERED THE COMPETITION.

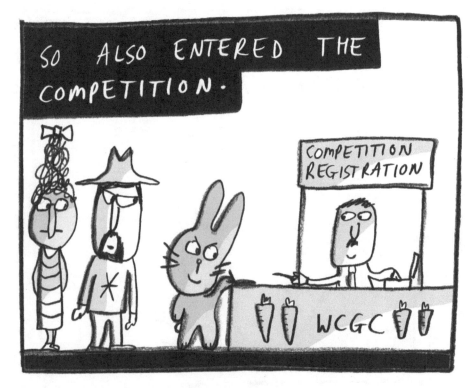

THE STARTING BUGLE SOUNDED.

PAAARP!

THE ENTRANTS RAN TO THEIR PLOTS...

PLOTS ▷

183

THEN, WHEN NO-ONE SUSPECTED ANYTHING, DEVIL-CAT BEGAN HIS MISCHIEF!

AND THEN HID IN A BUSH AND SPIED ON DEVIL-CAT.

BUT IT WAS HARDER THAN HE EXPECTED.

THE FIRST POTION MADE THINGS EXPLODE.

200

202

THAT NIGHT HE SNUCK OVER TO DEVIL-CAT'S HOUSE.

AND HE WAS RIGHT. BUNNY-FACE KEPT THE POTION IN A BACKPACK, WHICH HE NEVER TOOK OFF.

HE EVEN SLEPT WITH IT ON.

① I'll Pour some of the FAST-ShRINK INTO A BoTTle of FaRTY-COLa.

AND IF You DONT KNOW WHAT FARTY- COLa IS, THERE IS A WHOLE BooK ABouT IT (SEE VoLumE 2)

② FARTY-COLA iS A DELicious
COLA THAT MAKES YOU...
... HOW SHOULD WE SAY THIS?
A LITTLE <u>GASSY</u>.

③ I'LL SECRETLY LEAVE THE
BOTTLE AT BUNNY-FACE'S
PLOT.

PLOT
#175

⑥ iLL THEN JUST GO over, GRAB tHE BACKPACK ANd RE-CLAIM MY FAST-GROW POTION.

⑦ ANd THERE WiLL be NothING BUNNY-FACE CAN do ABOUT It.

FAST GROW

IN WENT THE FAST-SHRINK.

THEN HE TOOK A <u>MASSIVE</u> GULP.

HE <u>IMMEDIATELY</u> BEGAN TO SHRINK!

THE SIGHT OF A TINY BORIS WAS COMPLETELY HORRIFYING TO HIM.

IN HIS PANIC, THE BOTTLE OF FAST-GROW DROPPED OUT OF HIS BACKPACK.

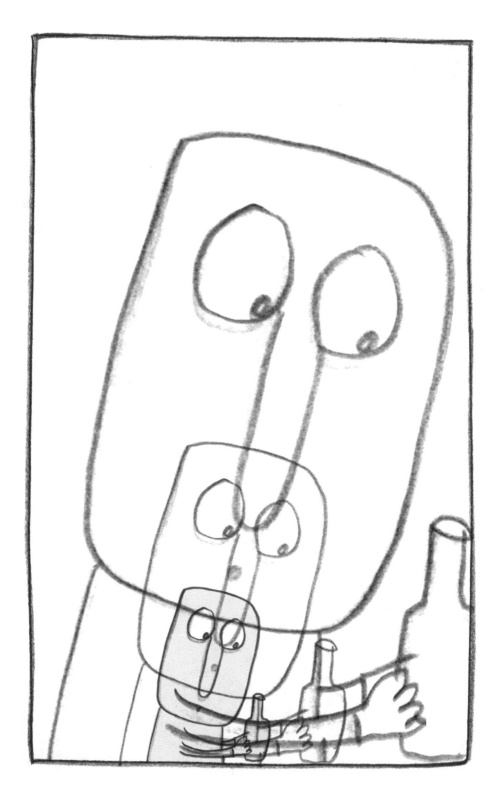

232

236

BRUNO THEN HEADED TOWARDS THE COMPETITION TENT.

DEVIL-CAT, MEANWHILE, HAD ARRIVED TO CHECK UP ON HOW HIS PLAN WAS GOING.
HE'D BROUGHT THE LAST OF THE FAST-SHRINK, JUST IN CASE IT MIGHT BE NEEDED.

WHEN HE SPOTTED THE GIANT BRUNO, HIS EYES ALMOST POPPED OUT.

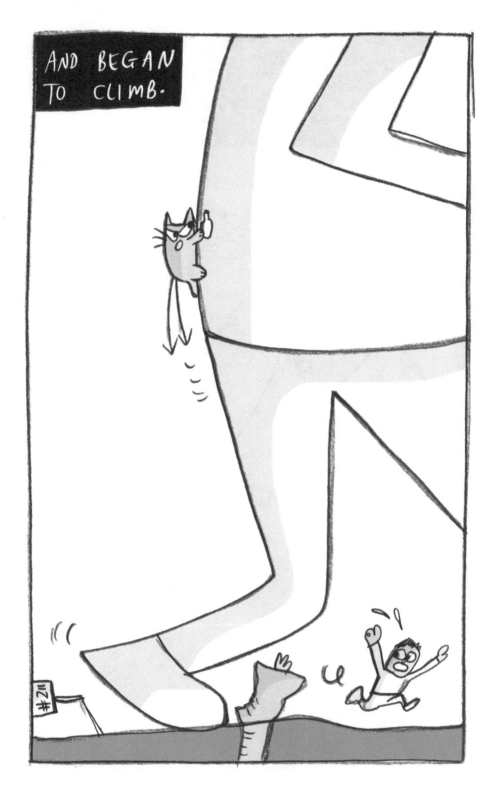

HE THEN LEFT THE SCENE VERY QUICKLY AND VERY CONFUSED.

... WITH A STILL-TINY BORIS SCAMPERING OFF AFTER HIM.

JOURNALISTS + CAMERAMEN ARRIVED.

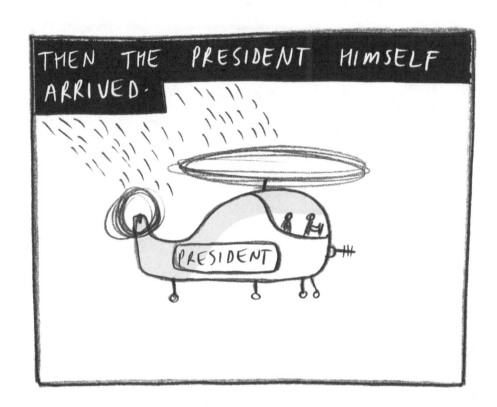

Do you want to know why Devil-Cat is *so scared of watermelons?*

The answer actually involves an exploding watermelon, but it's such a long story that it takes over 80 pages to explain!

You can read all about it in THE ADVENTURES OF DEVIL-CAT Volume 1, out now!

Smiley-Cola is the most popular cola on the market. But when Devil-Cat and Bunny-Face start selling their OWN concoctions, strange things start happening all over town.

Follow Devil-Cat's belly-busting adventures as he battles Bunny-Face for control of the milkshake market, and for glory in the World Carrot Growing Championship.

**Have you checked out our
TOTAL MAYHEM illustrated chapter book series?**

*Total Mayhem is a hilarious, action-packed,
highly-original series starring* **Dash Candoo** *and his
friends, as they battle the forces of evil.*

And Devil-Cat guest-stars in them too!

**Each book is a day of the week
and they are SERIOUSLY FUN!**

*"A high-octane caper"
– Publishers Weekly*

*"Delightfully chaotic"
– Kirkus Reviews*

*"Absolutely awful!"
– Mrs. Belch-Hick*

When ALL the world-famous Fluff-tailed Hemple-fluffer ducks
disappear from Zoo Lake, Dash and Rob jump into action.
They soon realise the ducks haven't just gone off on their own.
Instead, a MAJOR criminal operation (and duck-napping)
has taken place. They need to stop it, and fast!

*Something is amiss at the Botanical Gardens.
Does it have anything to do with the mysterious helicopter
landings on Norma Island? That place is STRICTLY OUT OF
BOUNDS, which is why Dash and friends need to get there
fast to investigate.*

The hatch was open and penguins were POURING out. "STAY CALM!"
yelled the principal, Mrs. Rosebank. "GO BACK TO YOUR
CLASSROOMS!" Dash and friends do as they're told, but when
something happens to their new classmate Ellen Ellenbogen -
linked to the world famous Ellenbogen Snausage Factory   -
it's time to act, and sneriously fast.

One of the most exciting events of the year is taking place at
Swedhump Elementary: Marble Day. When the grand prize gets
stolen and then recovered, it seems as if all is well. But then
things begin to rapidly unravel. Dash, Greta, Rob and Ellen
have another mystery to solve!

It's Kite Festival Swedhump Elementary, a fantastic annu-
al event with lots of prizes to be won. But just a few hours
before the opening, a terrible discovery is made. Dash and
friends need to get into action and solve the mystery, FAST,
before the festival is cancelled!

267

The world's FUNNIEST and also MOST USEFUL joke book EVER.

743 laugh-out-loud jokes and then a HUGE INDEX at the back so you can find a joke for any occasion.

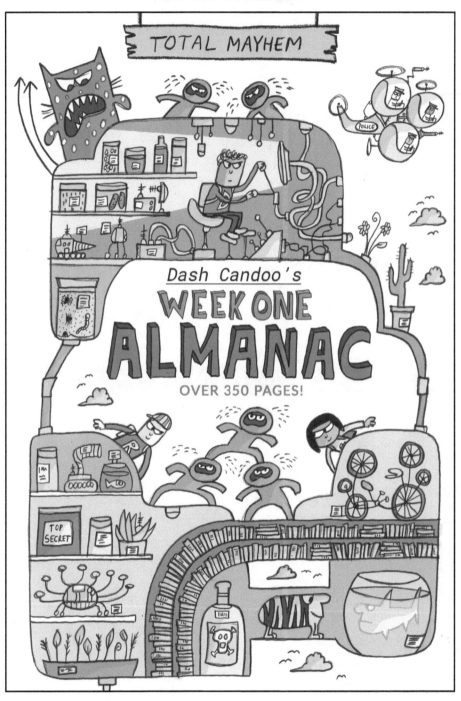

ONE MORE THING!

Did you know that we *self-published* these books ourselves?

Which is why they are only available on Amazon.

And so we want to ask you a *teeny* favor.

Actually a *teeny*, *teeny*, *TEENY*, *teeny*, *teeny*, *teeny*, *teeny*, *TEENY* one.

Would you mind writing a teeny teeny *review on Amazon?*

Or just give it a star rating. **Five stars** *if you loved it!*

Thanks. It makes a **big difference** to other people getting to hear about us. We really, *really* appreciate it.

No, we actually **really**, really, really, *REALLY*, *really*, really, REALLY, *really*, *really*, **really** appreciate it.

It's **REALLY** quite annoying how you repeat words like that!

One of my **main aims** in life is to be annoying.

In fact, let me revise that: One of my main, **main**, MAIN, *main*, main, *main*, **main**, main, **MAIN** aims in life is to be annoying.

Made in United States
Troutdale, OR
09/01/2024

22480859R10170